Mystery Structures from the

Written by Rob Alcraft

Collins

Mystery structures

All over the world strange stones and structures hide the secrets of the past. What can we learn from these mystery structures?

Remains like these hold the story of the past.

The secrets inside Egypt's pyramids

Egypt's largest pyramid was a king's grave.
Inside there are passageways and empty rooms.

Sphinx

hieroglyphics

Hieroglyphics reveal the pyramid's story.

Early pyramid explorers used dynamite to break in.

Now, new technology can see inside the massive structure without destroying it.

Will this lead to a secret passageway?

7

Tikal's lost temples

Something bad happened in Tikal 1000 years ago.

Causeways linked
temples and pyramids.

All the people left, and Tikal was covered by the jungle.

Workers revealed Tikal's ruins.

9

Why was Tikal abandoned? Experts suggest that people left because of disease and lack of food.

Tikal had skilled architects and stone carvers.

a carved stone figure

hieroglyph about a battle

Stonehenge mystery

Stonehenge has stood for thousands and thousands of years.

But it is a mystery how these heavy stones were transported here. When Stonehenge was made, people had no carts or wheels.

Some stones weigh as much as seven elephants.
It may be possible they were pulled from
a faraway quarry on sledges.

midsummer sunrise
at Stonehenge

Only very basic tools were available.

Nazca lines riddle

In Peru's Nazca desert, strange giant creatures are scratched into the dry ground. Why?

Layers of pebbles were scratched away to make lines.

a gigantic 2000-year-old whale

The Nazca lines only make sense from above.
Were they messages to sky gods, or important
symbols? The puzzle remains.

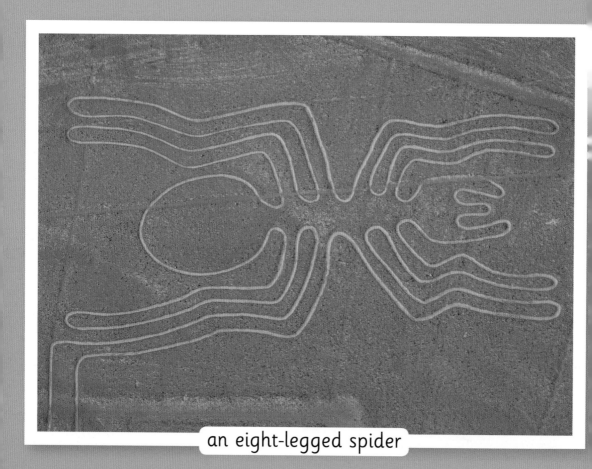

an eight-legged spider

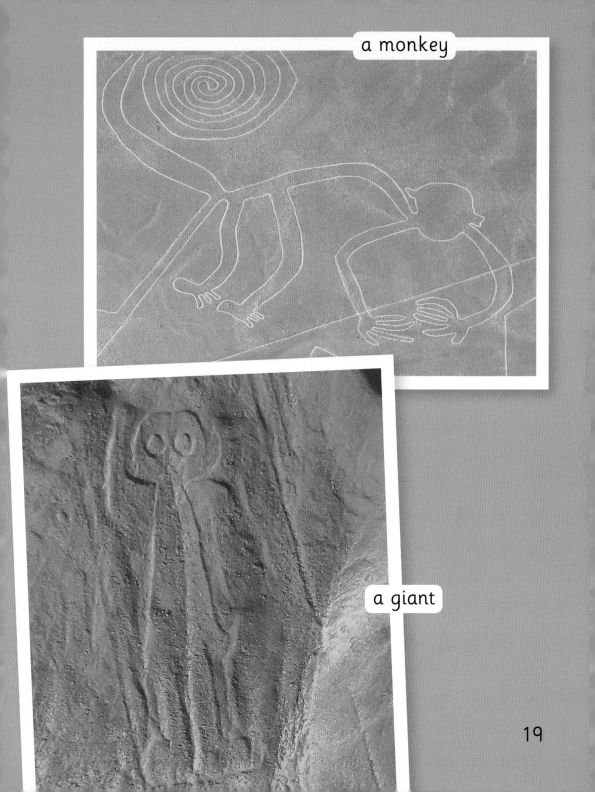

a monkey

a giant

19

Mysteries remain

Technology can solve some mysteries, but there are lots of things we still don't understand.

Why are these giants here?

What are these stone spheres for?

Spot the mystery details

❧ After reading ❧

Letters and Sounds: Phase 5

Word count: 300

Focus phonemes: /ai/ a, eigh /ee/ e-e, y, e, ey /oo/ u /igh/ ie, y /ch/ tch, t /c/ ch /j/ g, ge, dge /l/ le /f/ ph /w/ wh /v/ ve /s/ se /z/ se

Common exception words: of, to, the, into, are, were, people, because, break

Curriculum links: History: Achievements of the earliest civilisations

National Curriculum learning objectives: Reading/word reading: apply phonic knowledge and skills as the route to decode words, read other words of more than one syllable that contain taught GPCs; Reading/comprehension: drawing on what they already know or on background information and vocabulary provided by the teacher

Developing fluency

- Your child may enjoy hearing you read the book.
- Read the first double page then take turns to read a chapter. Challenge your child to read as if they are reading aloud on the radio. How interesting and mysterious can they make the structures sound?

Phonic practice

- Remind your child to break down longer words into chunks as they read these words. Tell them to look out for the different ways in which the /j/ and /c/ sounds are written.

architects	technology	messages
gigantic	passageways	

Extending vocabulary

- Ask your child to think of a synonym for each of the following:

riddle (e.g. *puzzle, mystery*)	gigantic (e.g. *massive, huge*)
faraway (e.g. *distant, far-off*)	skilled (e.g. *clever, trained*)
carved (e.g. *shaped, etched*)	strange (e.g. *mysterious, weird*)

Comprehension

- Turn to pages 22 and 23 and encourage your child to link the details on the right to the photos on the left.